PUFFIN BOOKS

A GINGER CAT AND A SHAGGY DOG

Ginger is a very mischievous kitten, and he's using up his nine lives fast. In fact, as he counts up all his narrow escapes, he realizes he only has one life left. Perhaps he'll be safe if he hides under the rhododendron bush? But no, adventures seem to happen to Ginger wherever he is!

Timmy loves Ginger, but what he really longs for is a dog. So when Shaggy turns up, with no collar to tell where he's come from, he can't believe his luck. A real dog to play with! Then his new neighbour, Sarah, comes looking for her lost dog, and suddenly Timmy must make a choice – to tell the truth and lose his new pet, or to tell a very big lie indeed.

Pamela Oldfield was a primary school teacher for ten years, but now writes full time. She is married with two grown-up children, and lives in Kent.

D1471952

STORNOWAY PRIMARY SCHO
JAMIESON DRIVE
STORNOWAY

STORNOWAY PRIMARY SCHOOL
JAMIESON DRIVE
STORNOWAY

A Ginger Cat and a Shaggy Dog

Pamela Oldfield

Illustrated by Linda Birch

PUFFIN BOOKS
in association with
Blackie and Son Limited

For Christina and William

PUFFIN BOOKS

Published by the Penguin Group
Penguin Books Ltd, 27 Wrights Lane, London W8 5TZ, England
Penguin Books USA Inc., 375 Hudson Street, New York, New York 10014, USA
Penguin Books Australia Ltd, Ringwood, Victoria, Australia
Penguin Books Canada Ltd, 10 Alcorn Avenue, Toronto, Ontario, Canada M4V 3B2
Penguin Books (NZ) Ltd, 182–190 Wairau Road, Auckland 10, New Zealand

Penguin Books Ltd, Registered Offices: Harmondsworth, Middlesex, England

First published as Blackie Bears by Blackie and Son Limited
as *Ginger's Nine Lives* 1986 and *A Shaggy Dog Story* 1990
Published in one volume in Puffin Books 1992
7 9 10 8 6

Text copyright © Pamela Oldfield, 1986, 1990, 1992
Illustrations copyright © Linda Birch, 1986, 1990
All rights reserved

Printed in England by Clays Ltd, St Ives plc

Except in the United States of America, this book is sold subject
to the condition that it shall not, by way of trade or otherwise, be lent,
re-sold, hired out, or otherwise circulated without the publisher's
prior consent in any form of binding or cover other than that in
which it is published and without a similar condition including this
condition being imposed on the subsequent purchaser

Contents

Ginger's Nine Lives

Ginger was one of those kittens who are always getting into trouble. One day, he overheard Timmy talking to Dad.

'I'm worried about Ginger,' said Timmy. 'I do wish he'd be more careful.'

Ginger didn't want to be careful. He ran into the garden and scrambled up into the pear tree to hide.

'Meow!' he cried. 'I'm so high
I can see over the fence into Mrs
Brown's garden.'

Timmy and Mum came out to
search for Ginger. Timmy looked
up and saw him. He and Mum
fetched a ladder and leaned it
against the tree. Mum held it
steady and Timmy climbed up.

Ginger went higher and higher.
Timmy couldn't reach Ginger so
he went down again.

Dad came out and they all
stared up at Ginger.

Just then, a blackbird flew into
the pear tree and perched on the
end of Ginger's branch. Ginger
began to creep along the branch

towards it but the blackbird saw him coming. It flew away so suddenly that Ginger was startled. He fell out of the tree and landed—plop!—right in the middle of a nice, soft bush.

Ginger was surprised to find that he was still alive. He

struggled out of the bush and
Timmy picked him up.

Dad laughed. 'It's a good thing
that cats have nine lives!' he said.

Ginger wondered about his
nine lives. 'If I only had one life,

I would have been killed falling out of the tree,' he told himself. 'But because cats have nine lives, I'm still alive. That means I only have eight lives left.'

He made up his mind to be more careful and he was —for a whole day! Then he forgot.

There was a fishpond in Timmy's back garden and Ginger liked to try and catch the fish. One day he stretched out his paw too far and overbalanced. SPLASH!

Luckily Mrs Brown was looking out of her bedroom window. She rushed round to Timmy's house and they fished Ginger out with a fishing net.

'That's another life gone,'
thought Ginger.

He decided to sit on the fence
and watch the cars go by. He was
so interested in them that he
didn't see a big dog coming
towards him. When it barked at
him, Ginger was frightened. He

leapt off the fence and ran across
the road! All the cars hooted
their horns. An old man on a
bicycle nearly ran over his tail,

but Ginger reached the other
side safely. The old man picked
him up and carried him back to
Timmy.

'Your kitten had a very lucky
escape then,' he said.

Ginger decided to find
somewhere safer. He went to

Dad's favourite chair, crawled under the big floppy cushions and went to sleep. When Dad came in from the garden and sat down he squashed poor Ginger flat! Ginger tried to meow but he could only squeak.

'Did you hear that?' cried

Dad. 'My cushion has started to squeak.'

Mum, Dad and Timmy all stared at the squeaking cushion.

Ginger popped his head out.

'Good heavens!' cried Dad. 'It's that kitten again.'

Ginger ran into the garden

and hid under the rhododendron bush. 'That's four of my nine lives gone,' he thought. 'Perhaps I'd better stay under this bush where I'm safe.'

Timmy found him there at

teatime and took him back into the kitchen. Mum was rolling out pastry and Ginger went under the table. He stretched out a paw and gave her ankle a friendly pat—but he'd forgotten to pull in his claws!

'Ouch!' cried Mum. She dropped her rolling pin. It landed on Ginger's head.

'Yee-owl!' he wailed. He ran out of the back door—and went on running.

At last he stopped and looked around. 'Where am I?' he

wondered. 'Where is Timmy? Oh dear, I think I must be lost.'

The little kitten *was* lost. For the next three days and nights he wandered along strange streets among strange people. He longed to see Timmy again—and he was starving.

Then, on the fourth day, he jumped over a fence—and stared round in amazement. He was back in his own garden!

'Meow!' he cried and a moment later he was in Timmy's arms!

They were all very pleased to have Ginger back.

Ginger soon found that he couldn't stop eating. He was so hungry after his adventure. He went into Mrs Brown's shed and ate a big piece of cheese that was lying there. Oh dear! Mrs Brown had put poison in the cheese to try and kill some mice.

That night Ginger had a bad tummy ache and by the morning it was much worse.

'We'll have to call in the vet,' said Mum.

The vet gave Ginger some bright green medicine. It tasted horrible but it made him better.

When Ginger was strong enough, Timmy took him into the garden.

'The fresh air and sunshine will do you good,' he said.

Ginger was feeling very worried. All he wanted was a nice quiet place where he could sit and think. When Timmy was not looking Ginger hid himself between the coal-shed and the garden fence. It was a very narrow space but Ginger squeezed in.

'Now,' he said to himself. 'How many lives do I have left?'

He counted.

There were only two!

Help! thought Ginger. He

tried to wriggle out of the little
space but he was well and truly
stuck. Now what was he going
to do?

It was Timmy who found
him. Dad was with him.

'That silly kitten,' Dad
grumbled. 'I'll have to take down
part of the fence to get him out.'

At last Ginger was free. 'I only have one life left!' he said to himself. 'I must find a safe place to hide.'

He ran down the garden and sat under the rhododendron

bush. Timmy tried to coax him out but Ginger had made up his mind to stay there.

Timmy had to take Ginger's food out to him under the bush. Every day Ginger ate his dinner and then washed his face. Then he sharpened his claws by scratching the stem of the bush.

One day Dad came down the garden with a clockwork mouse. He wound it up and it wobbled away across the grass.

Ginger was so excited that he nearly ran after the mouse. But he remembered just in time that he had only one life left! He shut his eyes and stayed where he was.

A week went by and still Ginger was afraid to come out. He sharpened his claws every day on the stem of the bush and each time the stem got a little thinner.

Timmy tried to tempt him with delicious food.

'Come out, Ginger,' he called. 'I've got a special treat for you. It's cod and double cream.' But Ginger remembered his ninth life and stayed under the bush.

One morning, Dad said, 'This nonsense has gone on long enough.' He marched down the garden and pulled Ginger out from under the bush. He carried him back to the kitchen and shut the door.

'If you play with him, Timmy, he may forget about the bush,' said Dad.

Timmy rolled a ping-pong ball across the floor and Ginger raced after it. Just then Mrs Brown came to borrow a cup of sugar. As soon as the back door opened Ginger rushed down the garden,

back to his rhododendron bush.

Soon even Timmy gave up trying to coax Ginger out and the kitten was very lonely. He stared out at the garden with his big golden eyes.

Sometimes Timmy came to talk to him.

Sometimes Ginger watched Dad weeding the garden.

Sometimes he saw Mum hanging out the washing.

He watched the birds hopping
about on the grass and once he
saw another cat.

Every day he sharpened his
claws on the rhododendron bush.
At last the stem was too thin to
hold up the bush and CRASH!
the bush fell down on top of
him!

'MEOW!' Ginger scrambled out from among the leaves and branches and stared at the bush.

'That was my ninth life,' he thought, 'but I'm still alive! IT'S NOT TRUE THAT CATS HAVE NINE LIVES. Dad was wrong!' And with a joyful meow he raced into the kitchen.

'Ginger's back!' cried Timmy in amazement.

They were all delighted.

Ginger didn't think Dad would be quite so happy when he saw the rhododendron bush.

'Never mind,' he thought cheerfully. 'Tomorrow is another day.' Ginger purred loudly and began to plan his next adventure.

A Shaggy Dog
Story

Timmy sat on the back step and watched Ginger. The cat washed first one paw and then the other. Timmy sighed. He loved Ginger very much but he did so want a dog.

'You see, a dog will run after a ball or fetch a stick,' he told Ginger. 'Cats don't do that.'

He wondered if Ginger would fetch something. After all, he was a very special cat. Timmy picked up a twig and threw it down the garden. Ginger ignored it and began to wash the tip of his tail.

'Just as I thought!' Timmy said, sadly. 'Dogs are different. You can take dogs for walks, and give them baths and teach them tricks.'

Ginger yawned to show that he thought dogs were boring.

'It doesn't have to be a big dog,' Timmy went on. 'A little dog would do.'

He went into the kitchen where Dad was peeling some potatoes.

'Are you sure I can't have a dog?' Timmy asked.

Dad smiled. 'No, no, a thousand times no!' he said. 'I've told you before, dogs cost money. They have to be fed and if they get ill you have to call in the vet. We can't afford vet's bills. But cheer up, Timmy. You've got Ginger, remember.'

'But he's not a dog,' Timmy muttered, so Dad couldn't hear.

Then he sighed noisily and he went into the front garden.

He stood on the bottom rung of the gate and looked up and down the road. A man walked past with a poodle on a lead and Timmy sighed again.

Suddenly, he saw an enormous dog hurrying along the pavement. It was black and white and very shaggy and Timmy thought it looked rather worried.

He called 'Here boy!' and the big shaggy dog rushed up to him. He wagged his tail and barked and jumped up and down at the gate.

'Are you pleased to see me, then?' asked Timmy, smiling

broadly. He looked over the gate, expecting to see the dog's owner, but the road was empty. He opened the gate and the dog bounced in and started to run round the garden. He was so big he made the garden look very small. Timmy looked for his collar but he was not wearing one. Timmy's eyes grew wider and wider. This dog was a stray.

'Come on, boy!' he shouted and ran to the back of the house. The dog ran after him and they both burst into the kitchen.

'Steady on!' cried Dad.

Mum was pulling on her wellies.

'Whatever's that?' she asked. 'It

looks like a walking hearth rug!'

'It's a dog,' said Timmy. 'A stray dog! And it's hungry. It wants a biscuit.'

'How can you tell?' asked Mum. 'It's so shaggy, you can't see its eyes.'

Carefully, Timmy tidied away some of the shaggy hair and they all looked at the dog's brown eyes.

'His name's Shaggy,' said Timmy.

'Oh, has he got a name on his collar?' said Dad. 'Maybe his address is on it, too.'

Timmy explained that he did not have a collar.

'Then how do you know his name?' asked Dad.

'I don't,' said Timmy, 'but it seems a good name for him.'

Dad looked at Mum.

'Look, Timmy,' said Mum. 'We can't keep him, so you mustn't get any ideas in your head. Someone must be out looking for him right now. It would be stealing to keep

a dog that doesn't belong to us.'

'But we could keep him just for tonight?' Timmy suggested, hopefully. 'In the morning, we could look for his owners.'

He was thinking that he could make a collar and lead out of string and take Shaggy for a walk. They could go to the park.

Shaggy could run after a ball, or fetch sticks!

'We really ought to notify the police,' said Dad. 'They look after lost dogs.'

Timmy was horrified. 'We can't do that!' he cried. 'They might put him in the dog pound. We might never see him again.'

There was a long silence.

Mum, Dad and Timmy all stared at Shaggy and he stared back, wagging his tail.

'You're right,' said Mum, at last. 'We can't do that.'

At that moment there was a rattle at the letterbox. It was Timmy's job to bring in the letters so he hurried up to the front door. Through the glass he could see the outline of the postman, so he opened the door. The postman handed him a small package.

'This won't go through the letterbox,' he said.

'Thank you,' said Timmy.

As the postman went out through the gate, a girl came in.

She was about the same age as Timmy and she looked very upset. She had ginger hair and grey eyes, and she looked as though she had been crying.

Timmy went down to the gate.

'My name's Sarah,' she said. 'I'm looking for my dog—'

Before she could say any more, Timmy said quickly: 'We have a dog called Shaggy.'

As soon as he said it, he felt terrible. He had told a lie.

'My dog's called Bruno,' she said. 'We've just moved into Number seventy-one and while the men were carrying in the furniture, Bruno ran away.'

Still Timmy said nothing. He

had wanted a dog for so long and now he had found Shaggy. He couldn't bear to let him go.

'He's a big dog,' Sarah went on. 'Black and white.'

Timmy heard himself say, 'Have you looked in the park?'

'I've looked everywhere,' she told him. 'I've been round and round the streets and Mum has phoned the police.'

'They might find him,' said Timmy.

His voice sounded different and he felt sort of shaky. He knew he ought to tell her the truth but if he did, she would take Shaggy away.

'I'll just have to keep looking,'

said Sarah. 'I'm so afraid he'll go
into the road and get run over.'

'I hope you find him,' Timmy
said.

He ran back into the house and
shut the door. He felt very
confused. It was all the postman's
fault, he told himself. If I hadn't
had to open the door to the

postman, I would never have met Sarah. Then I wouldn't know that she was Shaggy's owner.

She had seemed a nice girl and Timmy did not want to feel sorry for her.

He went back into the kitchen. Mum had broken up some bread and was mixing it with a tin of meat soup.

'If Shaggy's hungry, he'll eat this,' she said.

Timmy nodded. He gave the package to Dad.

'Oh good!' said Dad. 'It's the seeds I ordered. I'll plant them in the garden tomorrow.'

Timmy looked at him. Whatever would Dad say if he

told him about the lie?

Mum handed the plate of food to Timmy. 'You give it to him,' she said.

Without a word, Timmy put the food on the floor and Shaggy sniffed at it. Then he sat down and began to scratch his ear.

'You must eat,' Timmy told him.

'He's pining,' said Mum.

'He's not pining,' said Timmy. 'He'll eat it. I know he will.'

He knelt down on the floor beside the bowl of food and pretended to eat it, with loud gobbling noises.

'Yum, yum!' he said. 'What a delicious dinner. Meat and bread. How scrumptious. You'd better hurry up, Shaggy, or I shall eat it all!'

Shaggy watched him sadly. They tried everything they could think of but nothing they did would persuade him to eat.

Dad said: 'I know what we'll do. I'll write a notice and we'll pin it to the gatepost. We'll say we've found a dog and then if the owner is looking for—'

'If I had some string, I could take Shaggy for a walk,' Timmy said.

At the word 'walk' Shaggy pricked up his ears.

Dad found an old leather belt and made a comfortable collar for Shaggy to wear. He made a lead out of a length of cord.

'There!' he said, proudly.

Timmy tried to smile but his lips felt stiff. He wanted to get out of the house so that he could think.

He and Shaggy set off along

the road towards the park but halfway there Timmy had a dreadful thought: Sarah might be there, looking for Bruno.

'I'm sorry, Shaggy,' he said. 'We'll walk around the block instead.'

But suppose Sarah was still walking up and down the street?

'Blow it!' cried Timmy. 'Blow, blast and botheration!'

He went home again and Mum and Dad looked up in surprise.

'I've changed my mind,' Timmy told them. 'Shaggy might run away in the park. I think we'll play in the garden instead.'

Mum and Dad looked at each other.

'Is anything wrong, Timmy?'
Mum asked.

'No,' said Timmy and he
hurried out into the garden.

Ginger was playing on the grass with a dry leaf but as soon as he saw Shaggy, he ran up the pear tree. Shaggy lolloped after him, barking with excitement.

'Stop that!' said Timmy. 'Leave Ginger alone.' He found an old tennis ball and threw it down the garden. 'Fetch it, boy!'

Shaggy rushed after the ball and carried it back in his mouth. For the next half an hour they had a marvellous game and

Timmy began to feel happier.

When they went back into the kitchen they were both panting.

'Look,' said Dad and he held up a notice. It was written in red ink.

FOUND
LARGE BLACK
AND WHITE
DOG

'What do you think?' asked Dad.

'It's fine,' said Timmy.

Dad went into the front garden and pinned the notice to the gate.

When Timmy went to bed that night, Shaggy was put to sleep on a cushion in the kitchen.

FOUND
LARGE BLACK
AND WHITE
DOG

Timmy tried to get to sleep but
he was too worried. He thought
that Sarah might see the notice in
the morning and guess the truth.
She would tell Mum and Dad

and they would know about his
lie.

He lay awake, staring up into
the darkness. He thought it was
the worst night of his whole life.

Suddenly, he heard a strange
wailing noise and sat up in bed.
The noise went on and on.

Timmy had never heard
anything like it before but at last
he realized what it was.

Shaggy was howling.

Timmy jumped out of bed and ran downstairs.

Shaggy was standing by the back door, looking very sad.

Mum arrived in her dressing gown.

'I hope he's not going to howl
all night,' she said. 'We shan't get
any sleep.'

'Perhaps he's lonely,' said
Timmy.

'He's homesick,' said Mum. 'He misses his owners. How would you feel if you were lost and had to sleep in a house full of strangers?'

'Perhaps he would sleep better in my room,' suggested Timmy. He thought Mum would say 'No' but she said 'Yes'.

'Anything for a bit of peace and quiet,' she added.

Timmy took Shaggy upstairs and let him sleep on the bottom of his bed. Shaggy snored quietly but Timmy stayed awake for a long time, thinking.

It rained in the night and Dad's notice was ruined. The

rain had washed all the red letters
away.

'Oh dear,' said Mum. 'We'll
have to make another one. I'll do
it after I've taken you to school.'

Timmy finished his breakfast.

'Will Shaggy be here when I get
back?' he asked.

'I don't know,' said Mum.

Timmy said goodbye to
Shaggy and gave him a big hug.

He went to school and met
some of his friends in the
playground but he did not feel
like playing. He stood by himself
near the railings and was so busy

with his thoughts that he didn't see Sarah arrive.

'Hullo,' she said.

Timmy stared at her. 'Do you go to this school, then?' he asked.

'I do now,' she said. 'This is my first day. What's it like?'

'It's fine,' said Timmy.

She looked very nervous and Timmy felt sorry for her. She had just moved house and she had lost her dog. Now she was starting at a new school. He wanted to say 'Have you found Bruno?' but the words seem to stick in his throat.

Instead he said, 'I found your dog. I found Bruno.'

Sarah's expression changed at once. 'You've found him? How?

Where? Oh, thank goodness he's safe!'

She was smiling and Timmy smiled with her.

He felt a rush of courage. 'I found him yesterday,' he confessed. 'Before I met you.'

'Oh!' she said. She gave him a funny look. Timmy thought she would be angry but she just looked at him without saying anything.

He felt very hot and uncomfortable.

'I'm sorry,' he said. 'I should have told you yesterday.'

Sarah said, 'Never mind. You've told me now.'

'I took great care of Shaggy—I

mean Bruno,' he told her. 'Mum let him sleep on my bed because he was howling.'

She laughed. 'Did he snore? He does, sometimes.'

'Yes, he did.' Timmy sighed. 'I wanted to pretend he was mine, just for a little while.'

Sarah looked at him thoughtfully. 'We could share him, if you like.'

Timmy gasped. 'Share him? Do you really mean it?'

She nodded. 'We could take him to the park together and we could take turns to brush him. Having a dog is hard work.'

'If you were ill, I could look after him for you,' Timmy said,

eagerly. 'And I could buy him a
tin of dog food once a week out of
my pocket money.'

'You could take him for a walk
on Thursdays when I go to tap
dancing lessons,' said Sarah.

Timmy's mind was racing. 'I
could bring him to meet you from
the tap dancing class.'

'It would be fun,' she said.

They smiled at each other.

'We'll shake on it,' Sarah said. 'Like this.'

She held out her right hand and they shook hands. Then she held out her left hand and they shook again. Just then the bell rang and all the children stood still.

'What's happening?' asked Sarah.

'Another bell rings,' he told her, 'and we all find a partner and line up.'

'Oh, dear. I don't know anyone,' she said.

'You know me!' said Timmy, and they both laughed. They stood together in the line and

Timmy felt very happy.

He was not going to lose
Shaggy, after all. He was going
to share him with Sarah and that
was even better than having him
all to himself. He should have

realized that a dog like Shaggy
was too much work for one
person.

'I must remember to call him
Bruno!' he said and went into
school grinning all over his face.

Also in Young Puffin

THE TALES OF
OLGA da POLGA

Michael Bond

From the very beginning, there was not the slightest doubt that Olga da Polga was the sort of guinea-pig who would go places.

Olga da Polga is no ordinary guinea-pig: she has an extra special charm, a gleam in her eyes, a great personality and a very vivid imagination. In fact, for such a small animal, Olga gets into a great many adventures!

Also in Young Puffin

Adventures of ZOT the DOG

Ivan Jones

Life is fun with Zot!

Zot is a lovable little dog, and he and his friend Clive have all sorts of funny adventures. There's the cheeky mouse who plays tricks on them, a cunning snake who steals all the food, and an unhappy frog who does NOT like being swallowed up by Zot the dog!